Kangaroo
and cricket

Kangaroo
and cricket

Lorianne Siomades

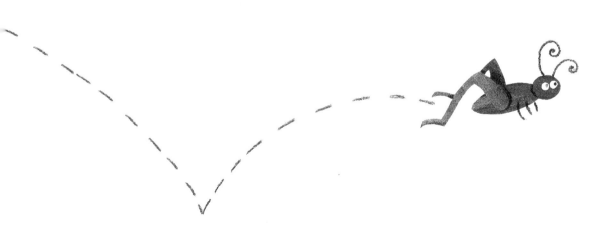

Boyds Mills Press

Kangaroo and cricket . . .
both can jump.

Camel and turtle . . .
both have a hump.

Whale and walrus . . .
both are big.

Badger and beetle . . .
both can dig.

Leopard and lizard . . .
both on a limb.

Fish and hippo . . .
both can swim.

Polar bear and penguin . . .
both can slide.

Bat and octopus . . . both like to hide.

Duck and dragonfly . . .
both have wings.

Dog and squirrel . . .
both bury things.

Crab and crocodile . . .
both can crawl.

Kitten and caterpillar . . .
both are small.

Pony and puppy . . .
both can run.

I have something in common

with everyone.

Published by Bell Books
Boyds Mills Press
A Highlights Company
815 Church Street
Honesdale, Pennsylvania 18431
Printed in China

Publisher Cataloging-in-Publication Data

Siomades, Lorianne.
    Kangaroo and cricket / written and illustrated by Lorianne
Siomades.-1st edition.
    [32]p. : col. ill. ; cm.
Summary: A book of opposites designed to show pre-schoolers that they
have something in common with everyone.
ISBN 1-56397-780-X
1. English language—Synonyms and antonyms—Juvenile literature.
[1. English language—Synonyms and antonyms.] I. Title.
    [E] —dc21 1999 AC CIP
Library of Congress Catalog Card Number 98-83074

First edition, 1999
The text of this book is set in 30-point Minion Semibold.
The illustrations are done in cut paper and watercolor and gouache.

10 9 8 7 6 5 4 3 2